A GIANT
THANK YOU TO:
JENNY, IZZY AND EMMA
FOR ALL YOUR
HARD WORK.

LIZ X

FOR HOLLY AND DAISY
WHO LOVE JELLY BEANS!

AND FOR DAD, HELEN
AND MUM

WITH ALL MY LOVE

X X X X X

First published in 2014 by Hodder Children's Books
This paperback edition published in 2015

Text copyright © Rachael Mortimer 2014
Illustrations copyright © Liz Pichon 2014

Hodder Children's Books, 338 Euston Road, London, NW1 3BH
Hodder Children's Books Australia, Level 17/207 Kent Street, Sydney, NSW 2000

A catalogue record of this book is available from the British Library.

ISBN 978 1 444 91040 7

Printed in China

Hodder Children's Books is a division of Hachette Children's Books.
An Hachette UK Company

www.hachette.co.uk

Jack and the Jelly Bean Stalk

by Rachael Mortimer

illustrated by Liz Pichon

Hodder
Children's
Books

A division of Hachette Children's Books

Jack's mum shook the biscuit
barrel and peered inside the bread bin.
She looked in dismay at the last few crumbs.

"I'm sorry Jack," she sighed,
"but the cupboards are bare and my purse
is empty. We'll have to sell Daisy."

"Don't worry Mum," said Jack, sadly.
"I'll get a good price for her."

Daisy was the cutest cow you ever did see. So it wasn't surprising that even before they got to town a farmer had offered Jack twenty gold coins for her.

"Twenty gold coins!" cried Jack. His mum would be so pleased.

Jack was on his way home when, all of
a sudden, he spotted a wonderful sweet shop.

Inside there were...

But Jack could not take his eyes off
an enormous bag of glittering jelly beans!

"These are magic beans, in every flavour you could wish for!" smiled the shopkeeper. "And for twenty gold coins, you can have them all!"

Jelly Beans
WARNING
may contain
smelly sock beans

AMAZING
Jelly Beans

TREATS

Every flavour he could wish for!
Jack couldn't help himself.
He handed over the money.

Jack walked home in a dream.
But when he arrived home without
Daisy and without any money
his mum was furious.

"You
silly boy!
What
use are
jelly
beans?"

She threw the bag outside and sent Jack straight to bed without any supper.

In the middle of the night, Jack woke to a delicious smell of...

...blueberries, chocolate, strawberries, ice cream,

and caramel wafting in through his window.

A **giant** jelly bean stalk was growing in his garden!

It was a beautiful sight – shining in the moonlight,
covered in brightly-coloured beans in all the yummy
flavours Jack had ever dreamed of !

Jack opened his window and began to climb, cramming jelly beans into his mouth as he went – orange, pear, mint, sherbet, choc-chip, apple pie, candyfloss, popcorn…

Higher and higher he climbed, until feeling rather full,
he came to a huge golden gate and a large sign.

GIANT JAM

Jack was hesitating when
he heard a strange noise.
He peered behind the door...

"Honk! Honk!" sobbed a little white goose. "The giant is so angry. I've tried my best to lay more golden eggs, but it's just no good! The pantry is empty, and there's nothing to eat in the castle except me and that stringy old harp!"

Suddenly, the ground shook!

Fee-fi-fo-foy,
I smell a juicy boy!
Goose is good but boy's so tasty,
Served with chips and wrapped
in pastry!

"Stop!" stuttered Jack as the giant scooped him up in his hand. "I'm very bony, and I haven't washed for weeks. Give me ten minutes and I'll bring you a banquet – a feast fit for a king!"

"Hmmm…" thought the giant, putting Jack back down again.

"My clock is ticking. Tick, tick, tick! Bring my feast and make it quick!"

Jack had never worked so
fast! In ten minutes
he had picked hundreds
of jelly beans.

The giant had melon beans for his starter and fish and chip beans for his main course. It was all washed down with a fruity bean smoothie. The goose watched hungrily.

The giant was just about to tuck into his pudding beans when...

...the goose swallowed
them down whole!

Honk!

The giant was furious!
He grabbed the goose
and shook her.

Honk!

Honk!

Honk!

But the beans would not come out!

He threw her down to grab his carving knife. Jack grabbed the goose and raced for the jelly bean stalk…

"Stop!" yelled the giant, thundering after them.

He grabbed the stalk and tried to climb down, but he was far too heavy. The jelly bean stalk began to sway. Jack jumped off just in time. It wibbled and wobbled...

...then came crashing to the ground far away from Jack.

CRASH!

Jack looked around and grinned.

Their garden was covered in jelly beans.

The goose never laid another golden egg. But she did lay delicious speckled ones, tutti-fruity ones, and tingy-tangy ones.

Jack and his mum had enough jelly beans to feed them for years! Although every so often they would find one that tasted like…